An I Can Read Book®

The Great Snake Escape

Story and pictures by Molly Coxe

HarperCollins*Publishers*

For Michaela, Conor, Eliza,
and all their friends who play in the park
—MC

This book is a presentation of Newfield Publications, Inc.
Newfield Publications offers book clubs for children from
preschool through high school. For further information
write to: **Newfield Publications, Inc.,**
4343 Equity Drive, Columbus, Ohio 43228

Published by arrangement with HarperCollins Publishers.
Newfield Publications is a federally registered
trademark of Newfield Publications, Inc.
Weekly Reader is a federally registered
trademark of Weekly Reader Corporation.

1995 edition

I Can Read Book is a registered trademark
of HarperCollins Publishers.

THE GREAT SNAKE ESCAPE
Copyright © 1994 by Molly Coxe
Printed in the U.S.A. All rights reserved.

Library Of Congress Cataloging-in-Publication Data
Coxe, Molly.
    The great snake escape / story and pictures by Molly Coxe.
        p.   cm. — (An I Can Read Book)
    Summary: Mirabel, a goose, and her friend, Maxie, a frog, get a
scare one day when a king cobra escapes from the zoo.
    ISBN 0-06-022868-7. — ISBN 06-022869-5 (lib. bdg.)
    [1. Geese—Fiction. 2. Frogs—Fiction 3. Snakes—Fiction.]
I. Title   II. Series.
PZ7.C839424Gr 1994   92-26528
[E]—dc20   CIP
                                                              AC

One morning Mirabel

went to see her friend Maxie.

On the way

Mirabel saw a page from a newspaper.

It said:

SNAKE ESCAPES FROM PARK ZOO

"Uh-oh," said Mirabel.

"I am afraid of snakes."

Mirabel ran to Maxie's home.

"Maxie!" she shouted.

"A snake has escaped from the zoo!"

"What kind of snake?" asked Maxie.

"I don't know," said Mirabel.

"Maybe it's a snake that eats geese."

"Or frogs!" said Maxie.

Now Maxie was afraid too.

Maxie hopped off her lily pad.

"Maxie, where are you going?"

asked Mirabel.

"I'm going to find a newspaper,"

said Maxie,

"so we can read the story

and find out what kind of snake it is.

Come on!"

Mirabel and Maxie saw a man
reading a newspaper.
The headline said:

BLUEJAYS WIN

GOMEZ HITS TWO HOMERS

"That's the wrong story,"
said Maxie.

The man turned the page.

The headline said:

SNAKE ESCAPES FROM PARK ZOO

"That's it!" said Mirabel.

Mirabel and Maxie read:

"Last night at feeding time,

a king cobra escaped

from the park zoo.

A king cobra is a long,

green and black striped snake

that eats . . ."

Just then the man stood up
and tossed the newspaper
into the trash can.

"Drat!" said Mirabel.

"We almost found out

what a king cobra eats!"

"We still can," said Maxie.

"You lift me up,

and I will reach into the trash can

and grab the paper."

"Okay," said Mirabel.

"Here we go."

Mirabel held on to Maxie's legs
and lifted her up.

"Can you get it?" asked Mirabel.

"Not yet," said Maxie.

Mirabel held on to Maxie's feet.

"Can you reach it now?"
asked Mirabel.

"Not yet!" said Maxie.

Suddenly Mirabel lost her grip.

CRASH!

"Maxie!" cried Mirabel.

"Are you all right?"

Maxie wiggled her arms and legs.

"I think so," said Maxie.

"Oh Maxie, I'm so sorry,"

said Mirabel.

"That's okay," said Maxie.

"I've found the newspaper.

Now we can find out

what the snake eats."

Maxie read out loud:

"Last night at feeding time,

a king cobra escaped

from the park zoo.

A king cobra is a long,

green and black striped snake

that eats other snakes and lizards."

"We are not snakes or lizards!"

Mirabel cried.

"Thank goodness," said Maxie.

"Now let's go home

and take a nice long swim."

Maxie tried to hop out

of the trash can.

"Uh-oh," she said.

"This can is too high.

I can't hop out!"

"Don't worry," said Mirabel.

"I will get you out.

I will push the can over."

Mirabel pushed,

but the can would not turn over.

26

"What are we going to do now?"

asked Maxie.

"I know," said Mirabel.

"I will find a stick

for you to grab.

Then I will pull you up."

"Hurry!" said Maxie.

Mirabel found a stick

and put it in the trash can.

"Can you reach it?"

asked Mirabel.

"No," cried Maxie.

"The stick is too short!"

"Drat," said Mirabel.

"I will try to find a longer one."

Mirabel looked and looked.

"I can't find a long stick anywhere!"
she said.

"What am I going to do?" cried Maxie.

"I will never get out of here!"

"Wait a minute!" said Mirabel.

"I know what we can use.

I have some string in my nest.

I will be right back."

BEEP! BEEP!

"What is that?" asked Maxie.

"It's the garbage truck!"

cried Mirabel.

"It's coming to pick up the trash!"

"Quick!" said Maxie.

"Get the string!"

Mirabel ran to her nest.

"Oh no!" she cried.

"This string is too short.

I need something long!"

"I'm long," said a voice.

34

"Who said that?" asked Mirabel.

"I did," said a snake.

He had green and black stripes.

"Don't be afraid," said the snake.

"I will not hurt you."

"I know you won't," said Mirabel.

"You're the king cobra.

My friend Maxie read about you

in the newspaper.

But now she is trapped

in a trash can on the hill,

and the garbage truck is coming!"

The snake started to slither away.

"Where are you going?"

asked Mirabel.

"I'm going to help

your friend Maxie,"

said the snake. "Let's go!"

Mirabel and the king cobra
hurried up the hill.

The garbage truck stopped.

A man got out.

"Help!" cried Maxie.

"Don't worry," shouted Mirabel.

"The king cobra will save you!"

The king cobra

reached into the trash can

and lifted Maxie out.

The snake took Maxie to a safe spot.

"Thank you, king cobra," said Maxie.

"No problem," said the snake.

"Now maybe you can help me."

"Sure!" said Maxie and Mirabel.

"Can you tell me

how to get to the harbor?"

asked the snake.

"I want to catch a boat

home to India."

"We will take you there,"

said Maxie. "Follow us."

Mirabel and Maxie

led the way to the harbor.

A rat showed them the boat to India.

"Have a safe trip," said Maxie.

"Thanks," said the snake,

"and keep out of trash cans."

"I will," said Maxie.

"Good luck!" said Maxie and Mirabel

as the king cobra

slithered up the gangplank.